Copyright © 2004 O Books
46A West Street, Alresford, Hants SO24 9AU, U.K.
Tel: +44 (0) 1962 736880 Fax: +44 (0) 1962 736881
E-mail: office@johnhunt-publishing.com
www.johnhunt-publishing.com
www.0-books.net

U.S.A. and Canada
Books available from:
NBN,
15200 NBN Way
,Blue Ridge Summit, PA 17214, U.S.A.
Email: custserv@nbnbooks.com
Tel: 1 800 462 6420
Fax: 1 800 338 4550

Text: © 2004 Marneta Viegas
Illustrations: © 2004 Nicola Wyldbore-Smith

Design: Nautilus Design (UK) Ltd

ISBN 1 903816 66 1

Printed in Singapore by Tien Wah Press (Pte) Ltd

relax Kids

Aladdin's Magic Carpet
and other Fairytale Meditations for Children

Marneta Viegas

Illustrations by Nicola Wyldbore-Smith

BOOKS

Winchester, U.K.
New York, U.S.A.

To all the children who have made me smile and
kept the child in me alive

To my family and friends across the world for their
constant love and support

To my Eternal Father, who teaches me every day
how to be silent and walk softly upon this earth

ABOUT THE AUTHOR

Marneta Viegas has been running her own children's entertainment business for eleven years. She co-founded the BlueTree Theatre Company, and every year she directs and produces a community-based theatre project — attended by thousands of children. She is also a talented mime artiste and has appeared at venues including Buckingham Palace in addition to working with village children in India.

Marneta has herself been practicing meditation for 23 years and has been teaching these techniques to both adults and children for over a decade. She currently runs RELAX KIDS workshops in London.

CDs

Sparkling meditations for shining stars of all ages
Fairytale meditations for princesses of all ages
Magical meditations for superheroes of all ages
Amazing meditations for wizards of all ages
Enchanting nature meditations for all ages

Cards

Star Cards — a treasure box of 52 cards to help children see and develop their inner qualities
Mood Cards — 52 cards to help children create positive moods and states of mind

For more information about RELAX KIDS visit:
www.relaxkids.com

8

CONTENTS

AUTHOR'S NOTE

I wrote most of the meditations for this book in March 2002 at dawn, sitting on top of a mountain in India. The air was pure, the atmosphere cool and silent, and my mind was fresh and clear. With each word came a profound experience of peace and lightness. And, as I wrote the meditations, I seemed to travel into the fairyland I would like children and even perhaps their parents to feel when reading this book. It was a very special experience – one that comes only from a state of deep relaxation and silence. From that moment I knew what I wanted to do – show children how to relax their bodies and minds in a simple and fun way.

Like every child, I was always deeply fascinated by fairy stories, and more recently they have played a major part in my work, both as a children's entertainer and a children's theatre director. I think the reason we are so attracted to fairy stories is that they touch something deep inside us. Within each story lies our deepest desire for ultimate love, happiness, and truth. From a young age, we yearn to live a life full of magic, where all our wishes and dreams come true.

Children love fairy stories. This is because they take the imagination to greater depths as they describe a world of exciting lands full of new possibilities. The characters often show either great feats of strength and incredible courage or acts of love and generosity. There is always the struggle of good over evil.

Fairy stories touch the very core of the human heart, because they speak to our deep and innate positive qualities and all that we strive to bring into our lives. I have found that the key qualities which run through most fairy stories are peace, love and happiness – the three things that everyone wants. I have

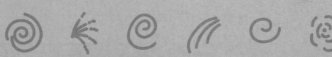

therefore based most of the meditations on these three qualities to give children an opportunity to dwell on them.

Transforming these well-loved fairy stories into simple visualizations gives children (and adults) an opportunity to taste the magic, as they explore the well of positive and pure feeling inside them.

Most little girls dream of being a princess or heroine with beauty and virtue, while most little boys desire to be a superhero with magic powers of strength and courage. By encouraging children to practice a combination of 'feminine' and 'masculine' meditations, they will have the opportunity to experience balance and a full spectrum of human qualities.

So, these story-meditations have been designed to encourage your child's imagination and creativity. In the process, I hope that they will lead the child into the same positive and peaceful emotional state that I experienced when I was seated on my mountain top in India.

FOREWORD

Aladdin's Magic Carpet is a magical book for you to read with your child at rest or bedtime. It is a gentle and fun way of introducing children to the world of meditation and relaxation.

With its colorful illustrations and easy-to-read narrative, taken from fifty two fairy stories and nursery rhymes, children are encouraged to go on magical journeys in their mind, identifying with the protagonist in each fairy story. The meditations or visualizations take all that is positive from children's favorite fairy stories, while removing anything that could potentially cause nightmares or restlessness.

Many children at the time of going to sleep are most awake. Just like adults, they suffer from over-stimulation. This book aims to counteract some of the tensions with which we are all familiar at the end of a busy day. They give children an opportunity to spend time with themselves and explore their inner world, alleviating anxieties and promoting restful sleep.

Sometimes the last thing you feel like doing is reading a story to your child at bedtime – which is why this book has been designed to give you space to relax alongside your child. The

affirmations at the bottom of each page are for parents to help create a suitable mind-set and atmosphere, thus aiding their child's relaxation as well as their own.

This book is also suitable for nursery and primary school teachers to read to children, as an aid to relaxation during quiet or circle time.

These visualizations have been tested on parents, children, and in schools, and the following benefits have been found.

Benefits for children:

bedtime becomes a fun and magical experience

children can sleep more peacefully

children are less likely to have nightmares, as the visualizations induce a feeling of calm and security

children develop confidence, imagination, concentration, creativity and self-awareness

children develop inner peace and a sense of inner security

children are more able to cope with the stresses of life, including tests of various kinds.

Benefits for parents:

parents will benefit from less stressful bedtimes

parents can enjoy better quality of life, as their children become less stressed and hyperactive

parents have a chance to relax alongside their child at the end of a busy day

parents have an opportunity to develop a strong bond between themselves and their child as they spend quality time together

Benefits for teachers/schools:

brings enjoyment to the classroom

children are more likely to concentrate on their work, as the meditations improve concentration and listening skills

the working environment of the classroom improves as children become more calm and focused

teachers are able to enjoy moments of peace and quiet, recharging their own batteries while the children relax

The affirmations, which have been included in each meditation for the parent/teacher, help to focus the mind and create a good atmosphere.

HOW TO USE THIS BOOK

For parents and teachers

Set the scene by playing some soft music. You may wish to pick a page at random, or take a page each day or week, moving chronologically through the book.

The affirmation which concludes each meditation is intended for the adult to use as a means of focusing attention and creating an atmosphere conducive to the children's concentration. *We recommend you read this first.*

After a moment's silence together, read the words slowly, with pauses, allowing the child to use his or her imagination.

You may like to read the words and then let the child drift into sleep, or you may discuss what he or she experienced, both in terms of what was visualized and the feelings which accompanied it. You may find that the child would enjoy comparing what is seen in the mind with the book illustrations.

ALADDIN'S MAGIC CARPET

Close your eyes, be very still, and imagine that you have Aladdin's magic carpet. Take a closer look: it is the most spectacular carpet in the world, made with very special golden thread. The carpet is colorful and has an exquisite design on it. Spend a few moments looking at the beautiful patterns and vibrant colors.

Sit in the middle of the magic carpet and cross your legs. Now say the magic word *Abracadabra* and feel the carpet start to float very gently above the ground. When you decide that you are ready to climb higher, the carpet will drift upwards. You will feel yourself getting lighter and lighter, as relaxed and happy as can be. The air is your home. If you would like to travel through soft downy clouds, you may do so, or you may ask the carpet to pick up a little speed and move forward. You know you are in control, and can choose to swoop and soar, zip and zoom, dip and dive, flit and flutter on this magic carpet. The tassels of the carpet are blowing in the wind. Feel the air rushing through your hair and the clouds brushing your face. You feel fresh and invigorated as the magic carpet takes you around the world.

Whenever you like, you may ask the carpet to slow down or float, as you stop to look at the beautiful landscapes below. You may wish to hover over the desert or the snow-capped mountains or the greeny blue sea. The choice is yours. Be free to go on your own special adventure and explore new and exciting lands and possibilities. When you are ready, ask the magic carpet to float back down to earth.

And now, when you are ready, wiggle your fingers and toes, have a big stretch, and open your eyes.

I AM FREE, I AM FREE

THE LITTLE MERMAID

Close your eyes, be very still, and imagine that you are a mermaid swimming in the clear blue-green ocean. As you swim, shoals of multicolored fish glide past, seeming to whisper a quiet *hello*. You can see a rainbow-colored fish in the distance, with his scales glimmering in the sea. You pass all sorts of weird and wonderfully shaped sea creatures in different colors. Can you see them? Crabs scuttle in the sand below you, sea horses glide regally past. You see a huge friendly and comical octopus dancing near his inky home in the coral reef.

If you want an adventure, you can dive downwards, right down to the bottom of the ocean. It feels so calm and peaceful swimming in the deep waters. You don't feel at all lonely, because you are surrounded by your fishy friends. You don't hear a sound, but just keep swimming deep into this peaceful ocean. With each stroke you feel as if you are becoming more and more calm and peaceful. You are afraid of nothing in the sea. The sea is your home. Keep swimming, becoming more and more silent and peaceful in your mind. Suddenly a dolphin offers you a ride. Thank him and climb up onto his back. Hold tight as he swishes through the water. Enjoy this feeling of riding through the ocean.

When you have had enough, slide off the dolphin's back and swim to a rock. Climb up onto the rock. Stay there for a while in the warmth of the sun. You may like to comb out your long hair as you sunbathe on the rock. While sitting there, continue to enjoy the feelings of peace you have created inside, as you soak up the sunshine.

And now, when you are ready, wiggle your fingers and toes, have a big stretch, and open your eyes.

I AM OPEN, I AM OPEN

ALICE IN WONDERLAND (1)

Close your eyes, be very still, and imagine that you are Alice in Wonderland. Look around you and you will see a strange land, talking rabbits, smiling cats, mad hatters ...

You find a little bottle of colorful liquid with a label saying *drink me*. You sniff the bottle and it smells like strawberry and chocolate and cherries. It smells so sweet and delicious. Drink the liquid. It tastes wonderful. You have never tasted anything so yummy in your life.

Very slowly you feel a lovely tingling in your feet. This feeling rises up through your whole body. It feels very warm and cozy. Then you notice you are very slowly getting taller and taller. You are growing, your head is going up and up and up into the sky. Your arms are growing longer. Your feet are growing too ... until finally you are so tall you can reach the sky. How does it feel to be so tall? Your head is peeping into the sky. It feels very peaceful and relaxing standing there with your head in the clouds. You feel the fluffy clouds brush past your cheeks. You can also feel the dewy mist on your eyelashes. You feel so relaxed and peaceful in the silent clouds – far, far away from the noise of the world. Stay there for a while, feeling peaceful.

When you feel ready to return to your normal size, take another sip of the delicious drink and slowly, slowly shrink back to your normal size.

And now, when you are ready, wiggle your fingers and toes, have a big stretch, and open your eyes.

I AM RELAXED, I AM RELAXED

PETER PAN

Close your eyes, be very still, and imagine that you are Peter Pan: you can fly. Just have one thought, *I can fly*, and then off you go into the air. You can twist and turn and whiz and spin in the air. Enjoy this wonderful feeling of being as light as a feather, as you soar through the summer air. You flit and fly, zip and zoom, dash and dart. Your wings are flapping powerfully as they take you further and further into the air. Sometimes you speed up and other times you slow down and enjoy gliding smoothly throughout the breeze. Fly as high as you wish in the air. When you are ready, gently land on a tree. Sit on a branch of the tree and be very still. Feel yourself swaying gently in the cool breeze. Stay there for a few more moments. Repeat to yourself *I am free I am free I am free I am free*. And now quickly fly into the air again. Spin and zigzag all over the wide blue sky. Fly up and over the fluffy white clouds. And now gently drift down onto a branch of the tree. Stay there for a little while, enjoying the soft swaying movements of the tree in the wind. Repeat to yourself again *I am free I am free I am free I am free*.

And now, when you are ready, wiggle your fingers and toes, have a big stretch, and open your eyes.

I AM FREE, I AM FREE

SLEEPING BEAUTY

Close your eyes, be very still, and imagine that you are Sleeping Beauty lying on the softest bed in the world. You have been asleep for a hundred years, and so every muscle in your body is totally relaxed and still. As you lie there, take in a deep breath and breathe out. Breathe in, breathe out. Each time you breathe in and out, you feel even more relaxed. You feel so warm and cozy, safe and protected as you lie there on your princess bed. Your body feels heavy on the feather pillows and soft satin sheets. Your arms feel soft and heavy, your chest feels soft and heavy, your tummy feels soft and heavy, your legs feel soft and heavy, and your head feels soft and heavy as you lie totally quiet on the most comfortable bed in the world. Breathe in and breathe out. Breathe in and breathe out. Each time you breathe in and out, you feel even more safe and protected, as you lie there on your bed in the castle. A forest of thorns has grown all around your castle and everyone else has been asleep for a hundred years as well. The entire palace is totally still and quiet. While you lie there asleep, you dream magical dreams of faraway places, fairies, dragons, unicorns, kings and queens. What are you dreaming about? Let your imagination be free, and dream your magical dreams.

And now, when you are ready, wiggle your fingers and toes, have a big stretch, and open your eyes.

I AM CALM, I AM CALM

JACK AND THE BEANSTALK

Close your eyes, be very still, and imagine that you have planted a magic bean in your garden. Look outside the window and you see the biggest, tallest, most gigantic beanstalk in the world. Go outside and stand at the foot of the beanstalk. Look up and see the leaves at the top disappearing into the clouds. You start to climb the enormous beanstalk. Further and further you go up into the air. If you have a look below, you can just about see your house. It looks very tiny from where you are, up in the air. Keep climbing up and up until finally you see the top of the beanstalk poking into the clouds. You climb right to the top and find yourself sitting on a soft fluffy cloud. You are so high up, all you can see for miles and miles are white clouds. It feels as if you are lying on mountains of cotton wool, they feel so light and spongy.

Just stay up here for a while, in the comfort of the soft and gentle clouds. You are drifting, drifting, drifting through the sky. You feel quiet and peaceful as you lie on these fluffy clouds. Your whole body feels soft and relaxed. Stay in the clouds for as long as you wish.

And now, when you are ready, you can start to slide at your own speed down the beanstalk. Sometimes you slide down fast, enjoying the feel of the cool air rushing over your body, and sometimes you slide down at a gentle speed, enjoying the view as you descend. Have fun sliding down the longest slide in the world.

And now, when you are ready, wiggle your fingers and toes, have a big stretch, and open your eyes.

I FEEL LIGHT, I FEEL LIGHT

PINOCCHIO

Close your eyes, be very still, and imagine that you are Pinocchio. You are made of wood. You are a wooden string puppet. Your body feels like a large heavy plank of wood. Feel yourself sinking into the bed or chair below. You are completely stiff, completely solid, and completely still. Your arms and legs are very heavy, because you are made of heavy wood. Your whole body is a big piece of wood. Stay there for a while, enjoying the sensation of being heavy. Let go and relax. Allow all the muscles in your body to let go, and sink deeply into your bed or chair. Your head is heavy, your tummy and back are heavy, your arms and legs are heavy. Stay there for a while in your relaxed and heavy position.

Now, very slowly, you start to feel a pleasant tingling sensation in your toes. Just like Pinocchio, you are becoming alive again. The tingling sensation is creeping up your legs and hips, chest, tummy, neck, arms, and head. Slowly you start to feel warm. Stay very still and feel your heart beating. You are no longer made of wood. Stay very still and listen to your breathing and just be very happy to be alive. Feel the blood pumping quietly through your body. Breathe in, breathe out. Breathe in, breathe out. Each time you breathe in and out, feel yourself becoming more and more alive.

And now, when you are ready, wiggle your fingers and toes, have a big stretch, and open your eyes.

I BREATHE SLOWLY, I BREATHE SLOWLY

MARY POPPINS

Close your eyes, be very still, and imagine that you are Mary Poppins. You can fly. Pick up your magic umbrella, open it, and hold it up in the air. Close your fingers on the comfortable handle of the magic umbrella, and let the wind take you up into the air. Just allow yourself to hang freely from the umbrella. As you dangle in the air, allow your body to totally relax. Let your feet relax as they sway gently in the air and let your legs hang. Let all the tension melt away in your legs as you enjoy this feeling of floating in the air. Let your arms and shoulders be relaxed. Enjoy the wind brushing against your face, relaxing your eyes, your ears, your forehead, your cheeks, your mouth. You feel as free as a bird. Don't worry or think about anything else, but just enjoy this experience of flying. Inside you feel so confident. The more confident you feel, the higher you can fly. You are so light and airborne that your arms will never feel tired.

Sometimes, the wind changes direction and you start to pick up speed and fly faster through the sky. It feels so exhilarating to be rushing and swooshing through the sky. Sometimes the wind dips and you drift down until it picks up again and sends you riding through the air at a brisk pace. Other times, the wind drops and turns to a light breeze, allowing you to float gently through the sky. It feels as if you are walking on air. Keep flying in the air for as long as you wish.

And now, when you are ready, wiggle your fingers and toes, have a big stretch, and open your eyes.

I AM CONFIDENT, I AM CONFIDENT

ALI BABA'S MAGIC CAVE

Close your eyes, be very still, and imagine that you are outside Ali Baba's magic cave. Just say the words *Open Sesame*. Suddenly, the walls of rock start to rattle and shake and a door magically opens. Go inside and you will see the most beautiful treasures: mountains of gold and silver, piles of glittering diamonds and sparkling jewels, and trays of precious pearls. Take a few moments to look around and investigate this cave of gleaming treasures. You feel so excited as you glance around this magical cave. In a dark corner at the far end of the cave is a dirty, rusty old lamp. Full of curiosity, you go to the lamp and pick it up.

Take the lamp, rub it clean, and as if out of nowhere a Genie appears. I am the Genie of the lamp. What are your wishes, O master? says the Genie. Now this Genie will not grant ordinary wishes. He will grant only special wishes. These wishes are wishes where you ask the Genie to change one thing you don't like about yourself. Maybe you're too impatient sometimes, or too noisy. Maybe you are a little selfish at times or get cross or upset. Whatever it is that you don't like about yourself, this Genie has the power to change it. Tell the Genie your special wish. He smiles back at you with an enormous toothy grin and answers *O Master, your wish is my command* and clicks his fingers. As you stand there in the dusty cave, you feel the magic working inside you. Every part of your body is filled with soft light. You are surrounded by stillness and peace. Stay very still, allowing the magic to work inside you. The part of your personality that you did not like has magically disappeared, leaving you feeling calm and quiet.

And now, when you are ready, wiggle your fingers and toes, have a big stretch, and open your eyes.

I HAVE THE POWER TO CHANGE,
I HAVE THE POWER TO CHANGE

THE MAGIC MIRROR

Close your eyes, sit very still, and imagine that you are looking into a magic mirror. Say to yourself *Mirror, mirror on the wall, who is the fairest of them all?*

Just stay very still and look into your reflection in the clear mirror, look into your eyes, and listen very carefully to what the mirror has to say back to you.

This is a very special magic mirror and it doesn't look at your features, but it sees the beauty inside your heart. The mirror is very wise and knows that having a beautiful face is not so important, as beauty on the outside can fade away. The mirror knows that true beauty is found inside. This mirror sees your inner beauty. It sees the beauty of your personality and your character.

Listen to the mirror whispering back to *you: you are beautiful ... you are beautiful ... you are fantastic ... you are special ... you are caring ... you are happy ... you are lovely ... you are clever ... you are wonderful ... you are fantastic ... you are amazing ... you are gorgeous ... you are strong ... you are lucky ... you are beautiful ... you are beautiful ... you are beautiful ...*

Can you hear the magic mirror saying anything else to you?

And now, when you are ready, wiggle your fingers and toes, have a big stretch, and open your eyes.

I AM BEAUTIFUL, I AM BEAUTIFUL

THE WIZARD OF OZ

Close your eyes, be very still, and imagine that you are walking along the Yellow Brick Road, on the way to visit the wonderful Wizard of Oz. You have a question in your mind that you would like the Wizard to answer. Have a think about what question you would like to ask the Great and Powerful Wizard of Oz.

Keep on walking along the road made of beautiful bright yellow bricks speckled with gold dust. Sometimes the road becomes very wide, sometimes it becomes very narrow, sometimes it goes over a bridge with a stream flowing underneath, sometimes it winds through a field of the brightest red poppies you have ever seen.

Finally you reach the magical Emerald City. The Wizard's palace is covered in tiny emeralds and is sparkling in the sunshine. Ring the doorbell and ask to see the Wizard of Oz. Go through the shimmering green door and follow the thick green carpet into a huge green room. You hear a voice: *I am the Great and Powerful Wizard of Oz ... What is your question?*

Ask your question and just be very, very still and quiet. This Wizard is always right and he knows the answer to every question. You have to stay there very still to be able to hear the Wizard's answer. Maybe he shows you something on his magic screen, which shows you the answer, or maybe he just says one word and you instantly know the answer to your question. Stay very still and watch and listen.

And now, when you are ready, wiggle your fingers and toes, have a big stretch, and open your eyes.

I HAVE ALL WISDOM INSIDE,
I HAVE ALL WISDOM INSIDE

THE TWELVE DANCING PRINCESSES

Close your eyes, be very still, and imagine that you are a prince or princess. It is night-time and you are lying in your royal bed with satin and velvet sheets. Everything is very still all around you. You can hear the owls hooting outside. Slowly you get up and put on your most beautiful clothes, made with golden thread, diamonds and pearls. How do the clothes make you feel? Next put on your shoes. These are magic dancing shoes. Your feet begin to tingle. Now you are about to go to the secret ball. Creep through the secret door in your bedroom and follow the tunnel hung with colored lanterns that leads to the river. Get into the boat that takes you to the royal ball. Your feet can't wait to start dancing. As soon as you arrive at the grand ballroom, you start dancing. Your toes start tapping, the heels start clicking, and then off you go. The shoes are enabling you to dance up and down and all around. You can even dance on the walls and on the ceiling. Enjoy this feeling of being so joyful, dancing with other princes and princesses. Your body is twisting and turning, leaping and galloping, tapping and clicking, hopping and jumping. You feel so wonderfully full of energy. Spend as much time as you like, dancing in this ballroom.

And now, when you have had enough for one day, you just clap your hands and the shoes will slow down and finally stop. Come out of the great ballroom and get in the boat that leads to the brightly-lit tunnel that takes you back to your bedroom. When you are ready, get back between the satin sheets and enjoy the feeling of being still again.

And now, when you are ready, wiggle your fingers and toes, have a big stretch, and open your eyes.

IAM FULL OF JOY, I AM FULL OF JOY

THE SNOWMAN

Close your eyes, be very still, and imagine that you are a snowman standing in the middle of a sparkling snowy garden. Everywhere you look is covered in crisp white snow. The sun is shining, making the snow glisten brightly. You are a snowman standing in the snow, with a carrot for your nose, stones for your eyes, and sticks for your arms. You are wearing a brightly colored hat and stripy scarf. A snowman can't move at all, so don't forget to be as still as you possibly can. Feel as if you are frozen right through, completely stiff.

A robin hops along the glittering garden, making tiny patterns in the powdery snow as he bobs along. Suddenly, he flies up and perches on your stick arm. Stay very still as he confidently hops up and down your arm. In a moment he takes flight, and off he goes silently into the wintry air. You are alone again; it feels good to be alone in this sparkling snowy garden. You like being quiet, you like being still.

While you are standing in the garden, take a few seconds to feel how peaceful it is on this sunny morning. The sunbeams are casting shadows on your snowy form – you are truly glistening and twinkling like thousands of tiny crystals. Feel the warmth of the sun on your frozen head and body. Very slowly feel yourself melting. Starting from your head, feel the snow melting and dripping down to the frozen ground. And now feel your body getting smaller and smaller, delightfully warm, and ready to move again. As each bit of snow melts, your body is transformed until there is only a pile of fluffy snow in the middle of the garden. You feel very relaxed and still, no longer a snowman.

And now, when you are ready, wiggle your fingers and toes, have a big stretch, and open your eyes.

I AM STILL, I AM STILL

KING MIDAS

Close your eyes, be very still, and imagine that you are King Midas. You have been given a very special power. Everything you touch turns to golden light. Touch your head and feel it transform into light. Touch your arms and watch them change into light. Touch your tummy and legs and they too turn into sparkling light. How does it feel to have a body of light?

Now you can transform everything around you with your magic fingers. Just have fun experimenting with this new magical power. Touch the table and it turns into a table made of brilliant golden light. Touch the rest of the furniture in the room and soon the whole room is filled with this beautiful light. Even the carpet becomes light when you touch it.

Go outside and touch the grass and the trees and flowers, and watch them transform into dazzling light. Soon the whole world becomes a magical world of light. You can even touch people with this special power. Whenever you see anyone, just lightly touch their arm. All of a sudden they become happy as they are transformed into beautiful people made of golden light – like angels. Start with people you know – your friends and family – and then softly touch everyone around the whole world. The more people and things you touch, the more the world changes into a happier and more beautiful place. See how much you can touch with your magic fingers.

And now, when you are ready, wiggle your fingers and toes, have a big stretch, and open your eyes.

I CAN MAKE OTHERS HAPPY,
I CAN MAKE OTHERS HAPPY

TREASURE ISLAND

Close your eyes, be very still, and imagine that you are on an island. This is Treasure Island and somewhere hidden on the island is a chest filled with treasure. It is time for you to go on an adventure to find this hidden treasure. You have to climb mountains, swim through streams and lakes, and go through dark caves. Keep looking until you find the treasure. Where did you find it? Did you have to dig deep in the sand to find the treasure? Or was it hiding in a cave or behind a bush? You open up the chest and see that it is filled with golden treasure. You see glittering jewels and pearls gleaming in the hot sun. You see gold and silver plates, goblets and jewel-encrusted ornaments. You take a closer look and see that there's something even more special about this treasure: written on each item is a word: *love, peace,* or *happiness.*

Pick up a diamond with the word peace written on it. How does peace feel? Stay very still and feel peace. Now take a ruby with the word love written on it. How does love feel? Stay very still and feel love. Pick up a sparkly golden chain with the word happiness written on it. How does happiness feel? Stay very still and feel happiness. You have all these special qualities hidden inside you like treasure. You just have to think about them and they will be revealed on your face and in your actions. Stay there for as long as you can, full of peace, love, and happiness.

And now, when you are ready, wiggle your fingers and toes, have a big stretch, and open your eyes.

I AM SPECIAL, I AM SPECIAL

happiness

Joy

Peace

Love

ALICE IN WONDERLAND (2)

Close your eyes, be very still, and imagine that you are Alice in Wonderland. You are in a strange and colorful world where unexpected and peculiar things happen. In front of you is the most delicious-looking cake. It has a label on the side saying eat me. So you have a sniff and it smells wonderful. This looks like the most yummy cake in the whole world, so you eat it. Can you taste how wonderful it is ... full of chocolate and strawberries and cream and marshmallows and all the things you love!

Then very slowly you feel a magical tingling in your head. You start to get a shrinking feeling. It is very pleasant. You start to have this lovely shrinking feeling in your arms and legs and the rest of your body. Slowly you start to shrink ... smaller and smaller and smaller until you are no taller than the cake. Everything in the room seems huge now. You would have to climb the chair if you wanted to sit on it. Then suddenly you see a tiny door just big enough for you to fit through. So you go through the door and decide to have a magical adventure. What do you do on your adventure? Whom do you meet? Where do you go?

When you are ready, come back through the tiny door, have another nibble of the cake, and watch as you grow back to your normal size.

And now, when you are ready, wiggle your fingers and toes, have a big stretch, and open your eyes.

I AM RELAXED, I AM RELAXED

THE WISHING FISH

Close your eyes, be very still, and imagine you are lying by a river bank. The sun is setting over the river and the sky is filled with pinks and oranges. The water is shimmering like a thousand tiny lights. Everything around you is so still. You feel very calm and peaceful. As you breathe in, enjoy this deep feeling of peace moving through your entire body. Feel your feet becoming still, feel your chest and tummy becoming still. Feel your arms becoming still, and feel your head becoming still. You are completely still, as you sit peacefully by the riverbank.

All of a sudden, an enormous multicolored fish jumps out of the water and starts to speak: *I am a wishing fish, what do you wish for?*

Tell the fish your wish. You may wish for whatever you like: maybe you would like to be a king in a castle, or a wizard with magic powers, or maybe you would like to fly. Whatever is your wish, tell the fish. As soon as you have made your wish, he replies *Your wish is granted*, and off he jumps, back into the shimmering river. Be very still and enjoy your wish. How do you feel? Happy? Peaceful? Sit peacefully by the riverbank, dreaming of how wonderful your life would be if this wish came true.

And now, when you are ready, wiggle your fingers and toes, have a big stretch, and open your eyes.

I AM PEACEFUL, I AM PEACEFUL

SNOW WHITE

lose your eyes, be very still, and imagine that you are Snow White lying completely still in a glass case in the middle of the forest. You don't feel at all scared being alone in the forest, because you are in a very secure magic glass case. You lie there motionless, not moving at all. You feel very safe and protected in your glass case. As you lie there, keep your eyes closed and see if you can breathe in the fresh smell of the pine forest.

Because you are so still, you can hear all the sounds of the forest. You can hear the sound of the breeze moving through the trees. You can hear the birds in the distance, singing high up on the branches. You can hear the bees buzzing around the flowers, and if you listen very carefully you can hear the butterflies' wings flapping. Stay extra still and listen: you may even be able to hear the sound of the ants tip-toeing over the soil. You may even hear the rabbits twitching their noses and the deer chewing. Can you hear the drops of dew dripping off the blades of grass? The more quiet you become, the more you can hear all the secret sounds of the forest. Listen, and count how many secret sounds you can hear.

And now, when you are ready, wiggle your fingers and toes, have a big stretch, and open your eyes.

I AM PROTECTED, I AM PROTECTED

THE GIANT'S GARDEN

Close your eyes, be very still, and imagine that you are looking at a huge wall. Over the wall is the Giant's garden. It is the most beautiful garden in the world. It is a secret garden, which you may visit whenever you feel a little lonely. A long time ago, the Giant used to be very selfish and would not share his beautiful garden with anyone, but he became sad and lonely and so decided to invite children to play. Would you like to go inside and see this fantastic garden? There is a tiny door in the wall: can you see it? Creep through the door and enter into the secret garden. This is the most amazing place you have ever seen. There are huge trees to climb and big tree-houses to explore. You can see swings and ropes to swing on, slides to slide down, hills to climb and roll down, sand and mud to play in, and flowers to pick. As you marvel at this exciting adventure playground, you stop to notice the wonderful smell of freshly cut grass hanging in the air. You may spend as long as you like in this secret garden. You are very safe and there are lots of other children to sing and dance and play with, so you won't be lonely. When you have had enough playing for one day, say goodbye to everyone and creep through the tiny door once again, and come out of the secret garden.

And now, when you are ready, wiggle your fingers and toes, have a big stretch, and open your eyes.

I AM HAPPY, I AM HAPPY

THE GOLDEN GOOSE

Close your eyes, be very still, and imagine that you have been given a goose with feathers of real gold. The goose's feathers are sparkling in the sunshine. She is so bright, and looks as if she is made of pure light. You are very good friends and enjoy playing together. You run with the golden goose and play hide-and-seek. You can always find the goose because of her shining golden feathers. You try to play catch, but the goose is so quick you have to run fast to catch her. When you have finished playing, sit very still. The goose is sitting very still and is about to lay a golden egg. Be very still and wait for the golden egg to appear.

The goose stands up and shows you the most perfectly shaped glittering golden egg. Look at the egg gleaming in the sunshine. You have never seen anything so marvelous. The egg is so bright that it seems it too is made of light. This is a lucky egg. Put it in your pocket. There are very few people who have the good fortune to keep a lucky golden egg in their pocket. This golden egg will bring you luck wherever you go. Sit for a few moments and feel what it is like to be truly lucky. Being lucky means that you will always have happiness in your life. Enjoy feeling lucky and happy.

And now, when you are ready, wiggle your fingers and toes, have a big stretch, and open your eyes.

I AM LUCKY, I AM LUCKY

THE WILD SWANS

Close your eyes, be very still and imagine that you have a special magic power. Whenever you like, you can grow wings and transform yourself into the most beautiful swan. Just have the thought I want to fly, and you start to feel a wonderful tingling feeling in your body. Concentrate on your fingers and watch as they slowly start to feel very light. They are slowly turning into feathers. Now, feel this tingling feeling spreading through your arms as you feel them transforming into beautiful feathery wings. Now feel your neck becoming long and elegant, just like a swan's neck. Very slowly, you feel the whole of your body changing into a beautiful white swan.

When you are ready, flap your wings and feel yourself flying up into the air. As you fly elegantly through the air, feel the wind blowing right through your whole body. You feel so light and free. Feel yourself soaring through the air with the wind brushing over your face and neck. As you fly, you feel so relaxed. Every muscle in your body feels soft and relaxed. Look down below – what do you see? Enjoy the wonderful scenery as you fly over trees and houses, rivers and seas. Keep flying for as long as you wish.

And now, when you are ready, gently slow down and land softly. Watch as your wings transform back into arms and feel your body come back to normal.

ROBIN HOOD

Close your eyes, be very still, and imagine that you are Robin Hood, all alone in the middle of the forest at night. You are not at all frightened, as you are one of the bravest people in the world. Sit in the middle of the forest. You are surrounded by old oak trees and thick grasses. Take a deep breath and breathe in all the fresh smells of the forest. Stay very still and listen. Can you hear the owl hooting from the branch above your head? The forest is very still and silent, but if you listen very carefully you will hear all sorts of secret forest sounds. Can you hear the mice scratching in the undergrowth? Can you hear the leaves shaking in the night air? Can you hear the mole sniffing along his underground tunnels? Can you hear the birds lying in their nests, shaking their feathers and stirring in their sleep? Now look up at the velvety blue sky. Spend some time watching the twinkling stars. How many can you see? Do they make special patterns in the sky? Are they all the same size? Do some stars twinkle extra brightly? As you look up at the stars, you feel very relaxed and quiet. You feel as if you could lie there all night, looking up at the dark blue sky. As you lie there, enjoy the feeling of being completely quiet and peaceful. You are as silent as the stars.

And now, when you are ready, wiggle your fingers and toes, have a big stretch, and open your eyes.

I AM QUIET, I AM QUIET

THE GINGERBREAD MAN

Close your eyes, be very still, and imagine that you are the Gingerbread Man. You have just been baked and are lovely and warm from being in the oven. You have raisins for your eyes and nose and a cherry for your mouth. You can smell the rich spicy smell of freshly baked gingerbread. Now, just like in the story, run as fast as you can out of the door, down the path, and along the road. See how effortlessly your legs will carry you. You don't stop for one second but keep on running. It feels fantastic being out in the countryside. Run up and down grassy hills. As you run past quaint little villages, people come out of their houses and stop and stare at the runaway Gingerbread Man. You look over your shoulder and can see them behind you, rubbing their eyes in disbelief. You feel so free. Keep running faster and faster, faster and faster. You reach a stream and, without even thinking, you take a huge jump and fly through the air to the other side. All the time you are running, you smile and laugh and repeat to yourself I am free, I am free as a bird. Enjoy this feeling of being free, as you run through the countryside. And when you are ready, stop, sit down, and just be still for a moment. Let every part of your gingerbread body become completely still and quiet.

And now, when you are ready, wiggle your fingers and toes, have a big stretch, and open your eyes.

I AM FREE, I AM FREE

ALADDIN'S MAGIC LAMP

Close your eyes, be very still, and imagine that you are holding Aladdin's lamp. On the outside, it looks like a rusty, dusty old lamp, but you know this is a special magic lamp. Inside the lamp there is a magical Genie who will grant you three wishes. Rub the magic lamp and watch the multicolored smoke swirl out. You see a Genie appear before your very eyes. He is wearing the most exotic satin costume, with a bright blue turban covered in precious jewels, and enormous gold earrings. The Genie folds his arms and asks in a deep voice *What is your wish, O master?* You have a chance to have three wishes. One for you, one for a friend or family member, and one for the world. Think very carefully now, as you have this chance only once, and you don't want to waste your wishes. Think of things that would make you and others really truly happy. When you have made your wish, the Genie says *Your wish is my command, master,* and waves his arms and shouts *Abracadabra.* Your wishes have now been granted and it's time for the Genie to return to the lamp, so off he disappears in a puff of colorful smoke. Sit for a few moments and think about how you feel, now that you have had your wishes fulfilled. Do they make you really happy? What does it feel like to have made others happy? What does it feel like to have done something good for the whole world?

And now, when you are ready, wiggle your fingers and toes, have a big stretch, and open your eyes.

I CAN MAKE A DIFFERENCE,
I CAN MAKE A DIFFERENCE

CINDERELLA

Close your eyes, be very still, and imagine you are Cinderella dressed in dirty rags. Your Fairy Godmother appears in a puff of pink smoke. She is wearing a stunning pink and silver lacy dress covered in tiny diamonds. She is holding a glittery magic wand in her hand. The Fairy Godmother sprinkles some magic dust all over you. As the sparkly dust falls all over your body, you start to tingle with happiness. Look down at your ragged clothes and watch them change into sparkling ones made of tiny stars. You are now wearing the most glorious dress of shimmering light. Your shoes are sparkling as well. They too are made of tiny glittery lights. You feel as light as a feather, in your outfit of white light. It is such a special feeling to be so light and sparkly. On your head is a crown of light. It sparkles like a million diamonds.

As soon as the clothes touch your skin, it is as if your whole body becomes soft light too. Just imagine that your arms and legs are made of light. Imagine your chest and tummy and head are made of pure light. You feel so soft and weightless. You feel like an angel. How does it feel to be light?

And now, when you are ready, wiggle your fingers and toes, have a big stretch, and open your eyes.

I AM LIGHT, I AM LIGHT

SINDBAD THE SAILOR

Close your eyes, be very still, and imagine that you are Sindbad the Sailor in a little boat on the ocean. The water is very calm, and you are gently bobbing up and down as the waves carry you along. Lie down in the boat and feel the sun on your face. You can smell the fresh smell of the sea air. The boat is quietly rocking from side to side. The breeze softly billows through the sails of the boat. You feel so free. Your body is relaxed; your mind is light. You are carefree, without a single worry in the world. Everything is quiet, apart from the sound of the waves lapping against the sides of the boat. You gently drift along the ocean to a desert island. Step out of the boat onto the softest, whitest sand. You can feel the warmth of the powdery sand between your toes. You are about to go on an amazing adventure on this island. You can explore wherever you wish on this island. You feel full of excitement as you prepare to explore this magical place. Maybe you find hidden treasure, or maybe you meet someone, or maybe you make a hut out of leaves and branches. You may even wish to have a dip in the ocean on this sunny day, or maybe you would like to collect some of the strange and wonderful shells on the seashore. Be free to have fun and explore this sunny island. And whenever you are ready to leave, step back into your boat and gently sail away. As the boat rocks from side to side, you gently breathe in and out, becoming more and more peaceful.

And now, when you are ready, wiggle your fingers and toes, have a big stretch, and open your eyes.

I AM GENTLE, I AM GENTLE

SOMEWHERE OVER THE RAINBOW

Close your eyes, be very still, and imagine that in front of you is the most beautiful rainbow. You can see reds, oranges, yellows, greens, blues, and purples in the rainbow. You have never seen such a stunning bright rainbow before. It makes you feel joyful and light just looking at it. You can see very clearly the beginning of the rainbow and so you decide to climb it. It is made of thousands and thousands of tiny multicolored lights. As you carefully climb it, one foot in front of the other, you feel full of excitement and anticipation. Where does the rainbow lead? You reach the top and you can see for miles and miles. The view is spectacular. What can you see? Stay up there for a while and enjoy the sights for as long as you wish. Then you decide to slide down the other side of the rainbow. It feels such fun. This is the longest slide in the world. Finally you reach the other side. What can you see on this side? Have you stepped into another magical world? Have you found the pot of gold? What do you see? Spend a few moments enjoying the world at the end of the rainbow.

And now, when you are ready, wiggle your fingers and toes, have a big stretch, and open your eyes.

I AM COMPLETELY HAPPY,
I AM COMPLETELY HAPPY

TOM THUMB

lose your eyes, be very still, and imagine that you are tiny just like Tom Thumb. Tom Thumb was only the size of a thumb and, because of his size, he found himself going on all sorts of exciting adventures. Are you ready to go on a great adventure like Tom Thumb? First of all, you need to sort out how to travel. As you are so tiny, you can climb up on a bird or butterfly and have a ride. Enjoy the feeling of drifting through the air as you move up and down gently. Feel the warm summer breeze on your face. It feels so wonderful to be alive and free. Then you decide to let go of the bird or butterfly and you start to float slowly to the ground. You see a field of green grass down below. It looks like a thick green carpet and so you know your landing will be soft and that you will be very safe. Enjoy the feeling of floating downwards through the air, letting everything go and being completely free. When you have landed, spend a few moments lying quietly in the soft grass before you continue with your adventure. Relax, relax, relax. Remember that the grass is much taller than you. It's like being in a forest. It's such fun being in this forest of grass. A friendly mouse goes past and offers you a ride on his back. Where does he take you? Spend some more time continuing your amazing adventure.

And now, when you are ready, wiggle your fingers and toes, have a big stretch, and open your eyes.

I ENJOY EACH MOMENT, I ENJOY EACH MOMENT

THE PRINCESS AND THE PEA

Close your eyes, be very still, and imagine that you are a princess who is lying on a bed made up of twenty mattresses. The bed is so high, you had to climb a ladder to get on top. The mattresses are made of the softest duck and goose feathers. Each mattress is so colorful, with its own unique and pretty design. You have brushed your teeth, combed your silky hair, and are now lying in your bed wearing your beautiful satin nightdress. You are lying down in between the smoothest silky sheets. Relax on the softest bed in the world, smelling the wonderful aroma of freshly washed sheets and lavender soap. Enjoy the feeling of your body sinking into the soft feathery mattresses. All your muscles feel completely relaxed. Take a deep breath in, and as you breathe out your muscles relax even more into the softness of the bed. Breathe in and breathe out. Breathe in and breathe out. Feel yourself go deeper and deeper into relaxation. As you breathe in, say to yourself I relax, and as you breathe out, say to yourself, I relax. Breathe in and relax, breathe out and relax. Now stay very still. Someone has put a tiny but very hard pea under the bottom mattress just to check if you are completely still and relaxed. Stay very still. Can you feel the tiny pea? Where has the pea been put? Where can you feel it?

And now, when you are ready, wiggle your fingers and toes, have a big stretch, and open your eyes.

I AM COMPLETELY STILL,
I AM COMPLETELY STILL

THE THREE LITTLE PIGS

Close your eyes, be very still, and imagine that you are one of the three little pigs sitting in your house made of the strongest bricks in the world. You feel so safe in this house. Lock the door and close the windows and sit down in the middle of this beautiful house. Allow your breathing to slow down; there is no need to be scared, because you are completely safe and secure in this house. Breathe in softly and breathe out softly. Breathe in slowly and breathe out slowly. Breathe in peacefully and breathe out peacefully. You start to feel very peaceful. As you breathe in, say the words *I am safe* in your mind, and as you breathe out repeat the words *I am safe*. This is your very special safe house, where nothing can harm or hurt you. The walls are so strong. You feel so safe here. Stay still for as long as you can, enjoying this feeling of safety and deep security. You can come here any time when you feel unsafe or confused or troubled.

And now, when you are ready, wiggle your fingers and toes, have a big stretch, and open your eyes.

I AM SAFE, I AM SAFE

THE MAGIC FLUTE

Close your eyes, be very still, and imagine that you can hear the most enchanting music far away in the distance. You go to look, and see it is the Magic Flute. You can see the Magic Flute glittering in the sunlight. As he plays, he skips along the path. You look again and see hundreds of boys and girls dancing merrily along behind the Magic Flute. They look so happy as they chat and sing and dance in the bright sunshine. *Where are they going?* you wonder. The happy procession dances past you, and the enchanting flute music makes you feel like dancing and joining in the fun. You see all your friends hopping and skipping and jumping away. You have never seen them look so happy. The Magic Flute leads all of you to a peaceful mountain. There is a little door in the mountain. The Magic Flute goes inside first and you all follow. You notice how still and peaceful you feel inside this mountain. The Magic Flute stops playing and all the children quietly sit down and are still for a few moments. How long can you be totally still for? Just keep repeating to yourself *It feels good to be calm. I enjoy being peaceful. I like being silent. I like being still. I like being peaceful.*

When you are ready, creep out through the door in the mountain and walk along the country path.

And now, when you are ready, wiggle your fingers and toes, have a big stretch, and open your eyes.

I AM PEACEFUL, I AM PEACEFUL

GOLDILOCKS

Close your eyes, be very still, and imagine that you are in the woods. Suddenly you come across a little cottage. This is the house of the Three Bears. Knock at the door – there is no reply – maybe the bears have gone for a walk, waiting for their porridge to cool down. Step into the cottage and walk into the kitchen, where you can see the three bowls of steaming hot porridge on the wooden table. In the sitting-room, you can see the three chairs by the fireplace.

Walk upstairs into the bedroom and you will see three beds. You don't feel like sleeping, but you would like to sit in one of the chairs downstairs. Which one would you like to sit on? You don't have to worry: they are very strong and won't break.

Choose your chair. Do you choose the big one that is very tall and upright or the medium-sized one with the soft cushions or the smallest chair? Sit down and close your eyes. It feels so comfortable sitting here next to the fire. Spend a few moments watching the fire spit and crackle, and feel your whole body warm up as you sit close to the blazing flames. Feel your body relax into the chair. Let your legs relax into the cozy chair. Let the muscles in your back become soft and relaxed as you sink into the softness of the chair. Let your arms rest gently on the armrests and become soft and relaxed. Your head too feels relaxed against the spongy cushions. Let all tension float away, as you sit for a few more moments enjoying the peace and quiet of the Three Bears' house. Repeat to yourself *I am relaxed, I am relaxed, I am relaxed.*

And now, when you are ready, wiggle your fingers and toes, have a big stretch, and open your eyes.

I AM RELAXED, I AM RELAXED

THE UGLY DUCKLING

Close your eyes, be very still, and imagine that you are an ugly duckling. You don't look at all attractive with your messy and muddy gray feathers. All the other ducklings laugh at you because of your ugliness. How does it feel being teased by the other ducklings? You try to be very brave and strong, as you know you are beautiful inside. You creep under your mother duck and feel safe and warm. Repeat to yourself *I am beautiful inside, I am beautiful inside.*

Then one day something strange happens. Your feathers change color and turn a brilliant white. Your neck becomes long and elegant. You have turned into the most beautiful swan. Stand next to the clear water in the lake and see your attractive reflection. Take a step into the water and start to swim gracefully. Gently glide along the cool water. You feel very peaceful as you swim in the tranquil waters of the lake. Repeat to yourself in your mind *I am beautiful, I am beautiful.* Really feel what it is like to be beautiful. It feels so soft and peaceful.

And now, when you are ready, wiggle your fingers and toes, have a big stretch and open your eyes.

I AM BEAUTIFUL, I AM BEAUTIFUL

THE EMPEROR'S NEW CLOTHES

Close your eyes, be very still, and imagine that you are the Emperor of a gigantic kingdom. Today is a very special occasion and you will be leading a huge procession through the streets of your kingdom. You have called for two tailors to make you the most fabulous new clothes. You are very excited about your new clothes, as you know everyone in the kingdom will be looking at them. Finally, it is time to try on the clothes. When the tailors hold the clothes up, all you can see is light. You look at the trousers and they are made of the purest rainbow light. The jacket is the most spectacular creation you have ever seen, with thousands of tiny jewels made of pure light. Put on your clothes made of light. As soon as they touch your body, you feel a magical tingle all over. The new clothes of light are making you feel joyful and happy, as if your whole body were made of pure light. All your troubles and problems have been melted away in this light. These new clothes have completely changed your mood. You feel brave and strong and full of self-confidence.

So off you go down the street, leading the procession of musicians and dancers. As soon as the people see you in your clothes made of rainbow-colored light, they smile and cheer. No one has ever seen such a remarkable thing before. It is as if your body has disappeared and is just made of pure light. The rainbow light clothes are changing everyone's mood. Just by looking at them, people feel joyful. Enjoy moving around in your stunning new suit of light.

And now, when you are ready, wiggle your fingers and toes, have a big stretch, and open your eyes.

I AM LIGHT, I AM LIGHT

BEAUTY AND THE BEAST

Close your eyes, be very still, and imagine that you are Beauty, sitting in a garden of red and white roses. Everything looks so pretty and you can smell the glorious scent from the roses wafting through the air. This is the Beast's garden, and he spends much time here lovingly looking after the flowers. The Beast may not be attractive to look at, but on the inside he has a kind heart and is filled with a loving and generous spirit. Today the Beast is upset because he feels no one wants to be his friend, as he is so ugly. He feels sad and lonely. You see him outside, sitting on the wall, crying. Hold his hairy hand. You don't feel at all scared, because you know he would never harm you. He just wants to have a friend. Tell the Beast to imagine that he has a heart made of gold, and the kinder he is inside, the brighter it shines. The Beast's heart shines so brightly because of all the love and care he shows his flowers. Unfortunately, people don't see that: they see only his hairy face. They don't see his kind eyes and sweet nature. Sit for a while in the garden, imagining that you both have shiny bright hearts. Can you make your heart shine? The more we have good thoughts and feelings, the brighter our hearts shine. Slowly the beast starts to smile — he feels so much better inside. Your kind words and love have made him feel special. You both feel unique and special. Sit there for a few more moments, feeling special.

And now, when you are ready, wiggle your fingers and toes, have a big stretch, and open your eyes.

I AM SPECIAL, I AM SPECIAL

THUMBELINA

Close your eyes, be very still, and imagine you are tiny, just like Thumbelina. You are only the size of a thumb. You are wearing a tiny dress made out of a fluffy dandelion seed head, with a hat made from a bluebell. You love going on adventures. Today you are going to the river. Jump onto a leaf that is floating on the water and start to drift down the river. Look into the clear water and you will see brightly colored fish smiling back at you. You feel so free and happy as you float down the river on such a warm day. Suddenly a butterfly flitters down to visit you. He sits and enjoys the gentle ride on the river. You quietly sit and chat, as you both enjoy the gentle ride down the river. The leaf brings you safely to the water's edge. Say goodbye to the butterfly and watch him flutter off into the distance. Then a kindly toad comes along and offers you a ride on his back. Climb onto the toad's scaly back and off you both go. You enjoy the feeling of jumping in the air and then landing softly. Up and down you bounce. You feel so excited as the toad jumps steadily up and down whenever you ask him to. Stay on the toad's back until he brings you home. When you arrive home, you feel so tired, as you have had such a fun-packed and exciting day. Crawl into your tiny bed. Your bed is made out of a walnut shell with fresh rose petals for blankets and a tiny feather for a pillow. Lie down and feel the softness of the rose petal against your body and the delicate feather against your cheeks. The smell of fresh roses is hanging in the air. You feel so comfortable. You have had such a full and exciting day and now it's time to rest. The walnut shell bed rocks from side to side. Enjoy rocking gently from side to side, as you drift into a wonderful deep sleep.

And now, when you are ready, wiggle your fingers and toes, have a big stretch, and open your eyes.

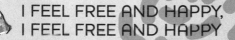

I FEEL FREE AND HAPPY,
I FEEL FREE AND HAPPY

THE HARE AND THE TORTOISE

Close your eyes, be very still, and imagine that you are a hare. You can run very fast, and so you have made a bet with your friend the tortoise that you will win the race. One, two, three, and off you go. You run so fast, you overtake the tortoise in a second. Enjoy this feeling as you bound through fields, speed up and down hills, and race down country roads. Sometimes you take enormous jumps to get you to the finishing line quicker. You love jumping: it makes you feel so alive and free. Just around the corner, you decide to have a little rest. Lie down in the sunshine and let all your muscles relax after being so energetic. Relax your legs, relax your tummy, relax your chest, relax your shoulders, relax your neck, relax your head. Just relax and drift off to sleep in the glorious sunshine.

Now imagine you are a tortoise in the race. You are very, very slow but very steady. Breathe in and out slowly, feeling very relaxed as you calmly plod through the fields, amble up and down the hills, and walk at a leisurely pace down the country roads. You feel so quiet and still inside, as you gradually walk along the path. Breathe in, breathe out. Breathe in, breathe out. Breathe in, breathe out. Take your time getting to the finishing line. Congratulations! You made it! You are the winner! You feel full of pride and satisfaction to know you are the winner. You took your time. You took your time, but you got there in the end. You can hear the soft snoring sounds of the hare in the distance.

And now, when you are ready, wiggle your fingers

and toes, have a big stretch, and open your eyes.

I AM SOFT AND QUIET,
I AM SOFT AND QUIET

THE SNOW QUEEN

Close your eyes, be very still, and imagine that you are standing in front of the snow queen. She has a beautiful long face, with jet black shiny hair and a white sparkling coat. She is covered in tiny ice crystals and has sparkly pink fingernails. She is glittering in the hazy sunshine of the wintry morning. She looks at you and gently smiles and then starts to blow her pure fresh, frosty breath over your face and body.

Slowly, very slowly, you start to feel your face becoming cool and still. Your neck becomes still, as the coolness of her breath touches it. Your arms become cool and still, your chest and tummy become still and finally your legs become still. You feel yourself becoming cooler and cooler. Feel yourself becoming stiller and stiller until you can hardly move. Just imagine you are turning to beautiful sparkling ice. Stay in your icy position for as long as you wish. How does it feel not moving at all? Do you feel peaceful? Do you feel still? Do you feel calm?

Now you see the sun rising higher in the distance. As the sun rises, you feel its warmth on your body and you feel grateful for the sun's rays. It is as if the sun is covering you in a warm blanket. You feel your body unfreezing again. You are slowly warming up and coming back to life. You can feel your heart beating and your breath is warm again. Take in a deep breath and breathe out slowly. Breathe in and breathe out. Stay for a few moments feeling very grateful for your body and your life.

And now, when you are ready, wiggle your fingers and toes, have a big stretch, and open your eyes.

I AM COOL, I AM COOL

JACK AND JILL WENT UP THE HILL

Close your eyes, be very still, and imagine that you are Jack and Jill walking up the hill. It is a beautiful day and you feel very happy as you skip up the hill to fetch your pail of water. Then, all of a sudden, you gently trip up. You feel quite safe, because the grass is soft and warm. Gently, you start to roll down the hill. Over and over and over you go, enjoying the ride. As your face touches the ground, you smell the richness of earth and the freshness of the grass. As your face looks up at the sky, you feel the sun's rays covering you. Keep on rolling, at a comfortable speed, accelerating as you go. You are getting faster and faster and you are full of excitement as you roll down the hill. Your limbs feel so loose and relaxed and your mind feels free. It is a wonderful feeling, rolling down this hill without a care in the world. When you reach the bottom of the hill, stay there in the sunshine and let your body come to rest. Enjoy the sun's rays on your toes and legs. Feel the warmth from the sun on your chest and stomach. Let your whole body become carefree, as the heat relaxes you. You feel so comfortable lying there, as sunbeams caress your face. Repeat the words *I enjoy being still, I enjoy being still.* Lie there in the warm sunshine on the soft grass, breathing in and out softly.

And now, when you are ready, wiggle your fingers and toes, have a big stretch, and open your eyes.

I ENJOY BEING STILL, I ENJOY BEING STILL

TWINKLE, TWINKLE, LITTLE STAR

Close your eyes, be very still, and imagine that you are outside at night. Lie down on your back and let your body become completely motionless. Don't move a muscle, but stay absolutely still. Keep your head still. Keep your arms still. Keep your chest still. Keep your tummy still. Keep your legs still. Keep your toes still.

Now look up at the dark velvety sky. It is so clear tonight, and you can see thousands of stars shining. Each tiny star is twinkling brightly. It feels so calming lying down and looking up at the stars at night. You feel very safe and secure. Each star up in the sky is different, as they all do different things. There is a peace star, a love star, and a happy star. Can you see them all? When you look at the peace star you feel so tranquil and silent inside. Stay for a while and look up at the peace star. Now look at the love star. You start to feel full of warm and loving feelings towards yourself and others. Stay for a while and look up at the love star. Now look up at the

happy star, and watch how you begin to feel light and happy. Can you see any other stars twinkling in the sky tonight?

And now, when you are ready, wiggle your fingers and toes, have a big stretch and open your eyes.

I AM A BRIGHT STAR, I AM A BRIGHT STAR

RAPUNZEL

Close your eyes, be very still, and imagine that you are in the tallest tower, just like Rapunzel. It is wonderful being so high up in the tower. You can see for miles around. You don't feel at all lonely, as the birds fly in to visit you every day. Each bird hops in through the window, bringing you nuts and berries to eat, and warbling their best songs.

You are standing right at the top of the tower, looking out of the window. The air is cool as it brushes against your face. Stay there for a few moments, with your eyes closed and the soft breeze touching your skin. Feel all the muscles in your face relax, as the wind touches your features. Your mouth and lips relax and become soft and still, your cheeks become relaxed and soft, your eyes become relaxed and your eyelids start to droop over them gently. Let all the muscles in your eyes completely relax and become still. Allow the cooling breeze to relax your forehead. Let all the muscles in your forehead become soft and relaxed. All the tension is melting away. Your whole face feels so smooth and serene. You feel so carefree and content. See how long you can keep your face completely still and relaxed.

And now, when you are ready, wiggle your fingers and toes, have a big stretch, and open your eyes.

I AM SOFT AND RELAXED,
I AM SOFT AND RELAXED

THE FROG PRINCE

Close your eyes, be very still, and imagine that you are the Frog Prince sitting right at the bottom of the deepest well that lies in a palace garden. It is very still in the well. It is very silent in the well. You like coming here to be alone and think. Outside in the garden, there can be lots of noise, and you can hear people chattering and calling as they play, but here in the well it is still and quiet. It is very deep and dark in the well, but you don't feel at all frightened or scared, because you know you can hop out whenever you wish.

Right down at the bottom of the well is some water. Now and again, you can hear the sound of water drops trickling into the well. Plop, plop, tick, tick. It feels very restful listening to these sounds. It is also very cool in your well. Outside, the sun is blazing, but the well is cool.

How still can you be in your well? If you are very still, you will hear marvelous echoes. Say the word *Peace* and listen to how the sound reverberates around the walls. Hear how the word *peace* gets quieter and quieter until it dies down and stops. Every time you say the word peace, really feel the meaning of that word vibrate through your whole body, right down to your bones. *Peace, Peace, Peace, Peace.* Can you feel peace in every bone in your body? You have to become completely still for this to work. How do you feel now? Do you feel peaceful? Do you feel calm? Do you feel relaxed? See how long you can stay totally peaceful without moving a muscle.

And now, when you are ready, wiggle your fingers and toes, have a big stretch, and open your eyes.

I AM PEACEFUL, I AM PEACEFUL

TINKERBELL

Close your eyes, be very still, and imagine that you are Tinkerbell. You are wearing a twinkly green dress with delicate transparent wings. You fly around the world, sprinkling magic dust and making all the children happy. It is such a big job, as there are so many children in the world. Flap your wings and start to fly. Enjoy this fantastic feeling of being free, as you fly over towns and cities. It is night-time and all the children are asleep, and you are like a tiny shooting star in the night sky. Enjoy the feeling of zooming and zipping, dashing and darting, whizzing and spinning through the velvety night sky. Spend a few more moments flying around the sky, shooting about like a tiny rocket of light. Now float down and delicately sprinkle your magic sparkling dust over children as they lie asleep, tucked up warmly in their beds. As the magic dust touches them, they softly smile. You enjoy dusting everyone with magic. It makes you feel happy to know that you are making other children happy. When you have sprinkled your magic over every child in the world, you can fly back to your home again, content and happy.

And now, when you are ready, wiggle your fingers and toes, have a big stretch, and open your eyes.

I AM FREE, I AM FREE

MAD HATTER'S TEA PARTY

Close your eyes, be very still, and imagine that you are in Wonderland at the Mad Hatter's crazy tea party. The Mad Hatter sits at the top of the table, pouring endless cups of tea from his enormous red and white spotty teapot. The March Hare is there, wearing a bow-tie and being very silly. The Dormouse has fallen asleep with his whiskers in his teacup. Tweedledum and Tweedledee are there, singing their favorite songs, as they roll around on their chairs. The Queen of Hearts is passing round her delicious jam tarts. The huge green caterpillar is there, talking to the White Rabbit, who keeps looking at his watch. The Cheshire Cat is sitting on the table, grinning his enormous grin. Everyone is dressed in brilliant-colored clothes. Everyone seems so happy. You feel so happy sitting at the party, surrounded by happy people. It feels such fun, and everyone is having a marvelous time laughing and joking and singing merrily.

The Mad Hatter offers you another cup of tea. With each sip, you feel more and more happy. This is such a strange but wonderful, wonderful Wonderland. Everyone is always so happy. The Cheshire Cat smiles at you with his pearly white teeth. Smile back. How do you feel when you smile?

This is a wonderful place, and the Mad Hatter has invited you to come back whenever you feel a bit sad or lonely, as he knows everyone will cheer you up.

And now, when you are ready, wiggle your fingers and toes, have a big stretch, and open your eyes.

I AM FULL OF HAPPINESS,
I AM FULL OF HAPPINESS

THE ELVES AND THE SHOE-MAKER

Close your eyes, be very still, and imagine there are some tiny elves that get to work as soon as you have gone to bed. Stay very quiet and pretend to be asleep. If you move one muscle they will know you are not asleep and won't come out. Are you still? Are you quiet? Breathe in and out very slowly. Stay very quiet; be very still. Through squinted eyes you can see these tiny little men creeping through the crack in the door. They are all wearing tiny little red and green jackets with matching shoes and pointy hats. They are so light on their feet, and look very happy as they skip into your room. Just imagine, you have your own personal little elves to do your tidying up. Stay completely still as you watch them clear things away, singing their merry songs and dancing their funny jigs. You almost want to laugh with happiness because they look so comical, but you must stay still or they will run away. When they have finished, they sprinkle magic dust over your whole room and then off they skip. The room is filled with sparkling magic. As soon as the magic dust falls over you, you begin to tingle all over with a wonderful feeling of happiness and gratitude. You feel very grateful to the little elves bringing a touch of magic to your room.

And now, when you are ready, wiggle your fingers and toes, have a big stretch, and open your eyes.

I AM GRATEFUL, I AM GRATEFUL

OLD MOTHER GOOSE

Close your eyes, be very still, and imagine that you are Old Mother Goose, riding a beautiful white goose in the air. This goose can take you wherever you like to go. Hold on tight to her soft feathery neck and off you go, speeding into the air. You feel so safe and warm riding on this enormous goose. You ride over mountains and fields, forests and rivers, oceans and deserts. You ride over the world. Look down below. What can you see? As you fly, you feel so open and free. You can feel the breeze touching your face and hair. Enjoy feeling the warm breeze gently touching your face. You feel like the master of the world. It is a wonderful feeling, flying across the world. Look down below again and see children looking up at you, jumping up and down and waving. They are so happy seeing you on your flying goose. As you fly over the world, repeat to yourself *I am free, I am free.* Fly for as long as you wish and, when you are ready, return home.

And now, when you are ready, wiggle your fingers and toes, have a big stretch, and open your eyes.

I AM FREE, I AM FREE

LITTLE BOY BLUE

lose your eyes, be very still, and imagine that you are Little Boy Blue asleep on a pile of straw in a barn. Everything around you is very still and serene. Your legs and arms feel so soft and heavy. Let them sink into the soft golden straw. Keep saying the words soft and heavy to yourself, and just allow your body to become soft and heavy. Say to yourself, *my legs feel soft and heavy, my chest feels soft and heavy, my tummy feels soft and heavy, my arms feel soft and heavy, my shoulders feel soft and heavy, my neck feels soft and heavy, my head feels soft and heavy.* Your whole body feels so relaxed now, lying on the soft warm straw. You find it is so easy to drift off to sleep here. Keep repeating the words soft and heavy and you will gently float into a beautiful deep sleep. Now you are free to dream magical dreams. What will you dream about? Where will your thoughts go? You can dream about wizards and kings, princes and pirates. Or maybe you would like to dream that you can fly? Just stay very relaxed and allow your thoughts to be free, and dream your magical dreams.

And now, when you are ready, wiggle your fingers and toes, have a big stretch, and open your eyes.

I AM COMPLETELY RELAXED,
I AM COMPLETELY RELAXED

THE OWL AND THE PUSSYCAT

Close your eyes, be very still, and imagine that you are sitting in between the Owl and the Pussycat. You are sailing the sea in a beautiful pea-green boat. It is night-time and the moon is shining bright. You look up and see thousands of twinkling stars, sparkling in the distance. The boat is rocking gently, and you can hear the soft lapping of the waves against the boat. Your heart feels so happy, as you lie there looking up at the stars. The coolness of the moonlight is touching you, making you feel very soft and peaceful. The wind is calm tonight and you can hear it whistling softly through the sails of the boat. The boat gently creaks as it sways from side to side. This gentle swinging motion is making you feel very sleepy. It feels so safe lying here in the moonlight. Let your body relax and be heavy. Let your legs relax and be heavy. Let your tummy relax and be heavy. Let your chest relax and be heavy. Let your shoulders relax and be heavy. Let your arms relax and be heavy. Let your head relax and be heavy. Let your whole body completely relax, and gently drift off into a dreamy sleep.

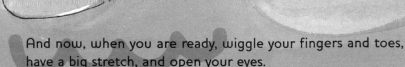

And now, when you are ready, wiggle your fingers and toes, have a big stretch, and open your eyes.

I AM CALM, I AM CALM

THE ENORMOUS TURNIP

Close your eyes, be very still, and imagine you are a tiny little turnip lying in the soft soil. It feels very silent here in the earth. You feel very still and quiet. You feel very still and quiet from top to bottom. How still can you be?

Now you start to have a tingling feeling all over. You are starting to grow. Feel your body expanding. The space between your top and bottom is getting bigger. Breathe in and out. As you breathe in, you feel yourself getting wider, and as you breathe out, you feel yourself getting longer. Breathe in, breathe out. Breathe in, breathe out. You are growing taller, lengthening and elongating, and growing wider and wider. Your whole body feels very relaxed as you are growing. Keep growing and growing and growing and growing and growing. See how big you can be. You are going to be the biggest turnip in the whole world. At any time, you may return to your normal size, because you know that you are in complete control of everything that is happening.

And now, when you are ready, wiggle your fingers and toes, have a big stretch, and open your eyes.

I AM RELAXED, I AM RELAXED

THE FAIRY GODMOTHER

Close your eyes, be very still, and imagine that standing in front of you is a glittering Fairy Godmother. She appears from thin air – whenever you need her to change your mood. How do you feel today? Are you sad or upset, cross or lonely, or just feeling tired? The Fairy Godmother can change your mood in a second. She tells you to sit down and close your eyes. She waves her magic wand three times and says *you are special, you are special, you are special* and then sprinkles sparkling glitter up in the air. Instantly, you have a magical feeling inside. You start to smile. Your eyes start to sparkle. Your face begins to look happy and radiant once again. The Fairy Godmother tells you to keep repeating the words *I am special, I am special, I am special*. As you realize how special and lucky you are, you start to feel more and more happy. The more you think about what you like about yourself and how special you are, the more the magic works and your mood completely changes. Stay there for as long as you wish, feeling happy and radiant.

And now, when you are ready, wiggle your fingers and toes, have a big stretch, and open your eyes.

I AM HAPPY, I AM HAPPY

THE FAIRY GARDEN

Close your eyes, be very still, and imagine that you are walking alongside a walled garden. You see a tiny door in the wall. Creep through the door, and you find yourself in a fairy garden. All around you, the fairies, pixies, and gnomes are busy at work. They are cleaning the garden. Others are gathering fruits and flowers. You see toadstools and magic fairy rings made with the prettiest flowers you have ever seen. There is so much color and life in this garden. Some of the fairies are dancing in a circle, singing joyfully. They invite you to join in their dancing. Round and round you go. It feels wonderful to be dancing with the fairies and pixies. Finally, you all fall to the ground and lie there for a while, in the softest grass you have ever felt. Enjoy this feeling of doing nothing but just soaking in the sunshine and enjoying being still and quiet.

And now, when you are ready, wiggle your fingers and toes, have a big stretch, and open your eyes.

I AM STILL AND QUIET, I AM STILL AND QUIET

THE QUEEN OF HEARTS

Close your eyes, be very still, and imagine that you are the Queen of Hearts. You rule a very special kingdom where it is the law for everyone there to be completely loving to one another. Imagine this unique world where hurtful words and unkind actions do not exist. Each person has only love and respect for everyone else. All value and admire one another. Just look at the expression on each one's face — everyone is so full of love that there is no room for any negativity or sorrow. Each one knows that they all have special qualities that make them unique and valuable. Do you know your qualities that make you special? What are you good at? What do people love about you? What do people remember you for? Think about your wonderful qualities for a few moments, and then watch how you start feeling. Are you starting to appreciate and respect yourself a little more?

And now, when you are ready, wiggle your fingers and toes, have a big stretch, and open your eyes.

I LOVE AND APPRECIATE MYSELF,
I LOVE AND APPRECIATE MYSELF